Larry Gets Lost
in Los Angeles

Illustrated by John Skewes
Written by Michael Mullin and John Skewes

SASQUATCH BOOKS
SEATTLE

Printed in China
Published by Sasquatch Books
Distributed by PGW/Perseus
15 14 13 12 11 10 09   15 14 13 12 11 10 9 8 7 6 5 4 3 2 1

Book design by Mint Design

Library of Congress Cataloging-in-Publication Data
is available

ISBN-13: 978-1-57061-568-9
ISBN-10: 1-57061-568-3

Larry adopts a food bank in every city he visits. A portion of the
proceeds from this book will be donated to a Los Angeles–area
food bank.

www.larrygetslost.com

SASQUATCH BOOKS
119 South Main Street, Suite 400
Seattle, WA 98104
(206) 467-4300

www.sasquatchbooks.com
custserv@sasquatchbooks.com

This is **Pete**.   This is **Larry**.

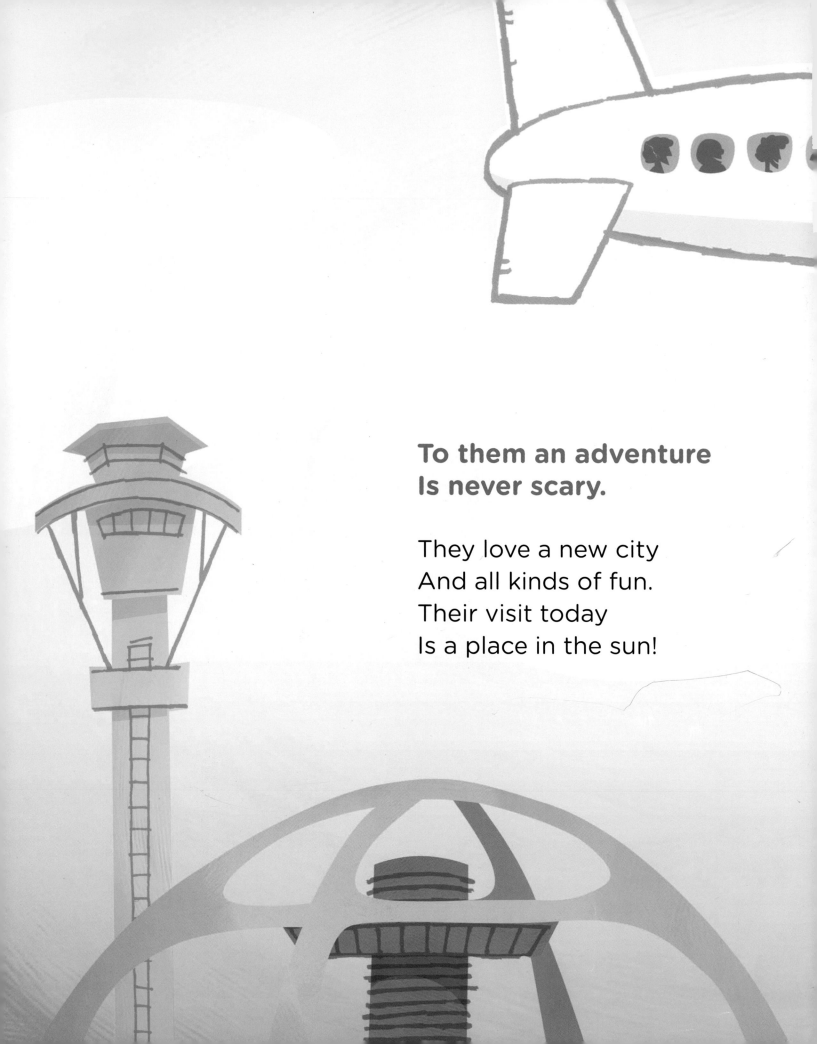

To them an adventure
Is never scary.

They love a new city
And all kinds of fun.
Their visit today
Is a place in the sun!

In the plane they were thinking about
Where they'd be next
When they landed near
An **"L," "A,"** and **"X."**

LOS ANGELES INTERNATIONAL
AIRPORT (LAX)

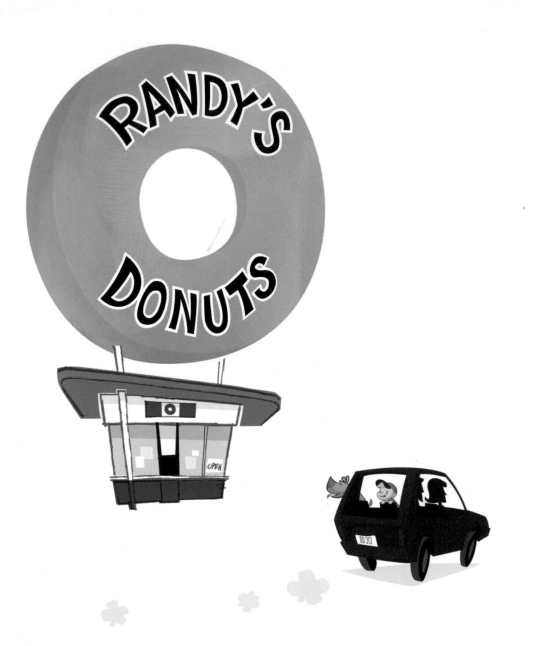

Outside Mom and Dad got the family a car . . .

**RANDY'S DONUTS,
INGLEWOOD**

L.A. FREEWAYS
The interchange between the
101 and 405 freeways is the
busiest in America.

. . . they drove for a while, **but didn't get far.**

There was so much to do
At the first stop they'd planned
It was some kind of magical,
Other-world land!

DISNEYLAND® RESORT
Disney's first theme park has
entertained children of all
ages for more than 50 years.

After riding and playing, they drove in their car
To a strange kind of pond, like a **big pit of tar.**

LA BREA TAR PITS
Animal bones and fossils—some over
10,000 years old—are discovered in the tar
every day!

From the grime of the tar,
Things got suddenly clean.
Every storefront and car
On this street was pristine.

"Kinda flashy," Pete said as
They wandered on through.
"And a bit too expensive
For me and for you."

What was this next place?
Larry could not tell.
It looked like musicians
In a **giant clam shell.**

Then they arrived at
A bustling place
Where wide-eyed wonder
Filled most every face.

HOLLYWOOD BOWL
Officially opened in 1922, the Bowl is an outdoor theater designed to fit into the hillside.

HOLLYWOOD

HOLLYWOOD BOULEVARD

sso & Frank Grill Since 1919

EAT
HOT DOGS

JOHNNY depp
16.IX.05
Marilyn Monroe
6-26-53
SHIRLEY TEMPLE
Aug 3 1977
R2D2

While looking at footprints of **famous feet . . .**

GRAUMAN'S CHINESE THEATRE
It's a tradition for movie stars to leave
their handprints and footprints in the
cement sidewalk in front of the theatre.

. . . Larry suddenly realized he wasn't with Pete!

On the sidewalk were stars, **each one with a name.**

Yet he saw no Pete star. So much for fame!

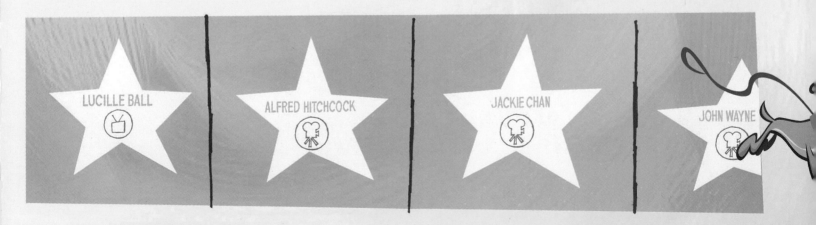

HOLLYWOOD WALK OF FAME
There are over three miles of stars along the sidewalk on Hollywood Boulevard and Vine Street, honoring stars of television, movies, music, radio, and theater.

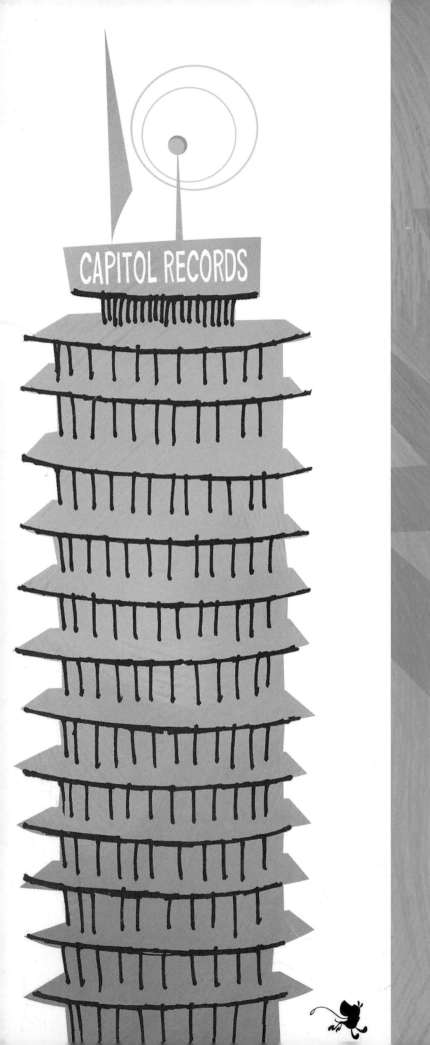

CAPITOL RECORDS BUILDING
A light on top of the building blinks
"H-O-L-L-Y-W-O-O-D" in Morse code.

HOLLYWOOD SIGN
The 50-foot letters originally read "Hollywoodland." It was shortened to "Hollywood" in 1949.

A **huge sign** seemed to give Larry a clue.
But a dog can't read. So what could he do?

He passed a **tall building**
That looked like a stack.
And wondered, was he on the right track?

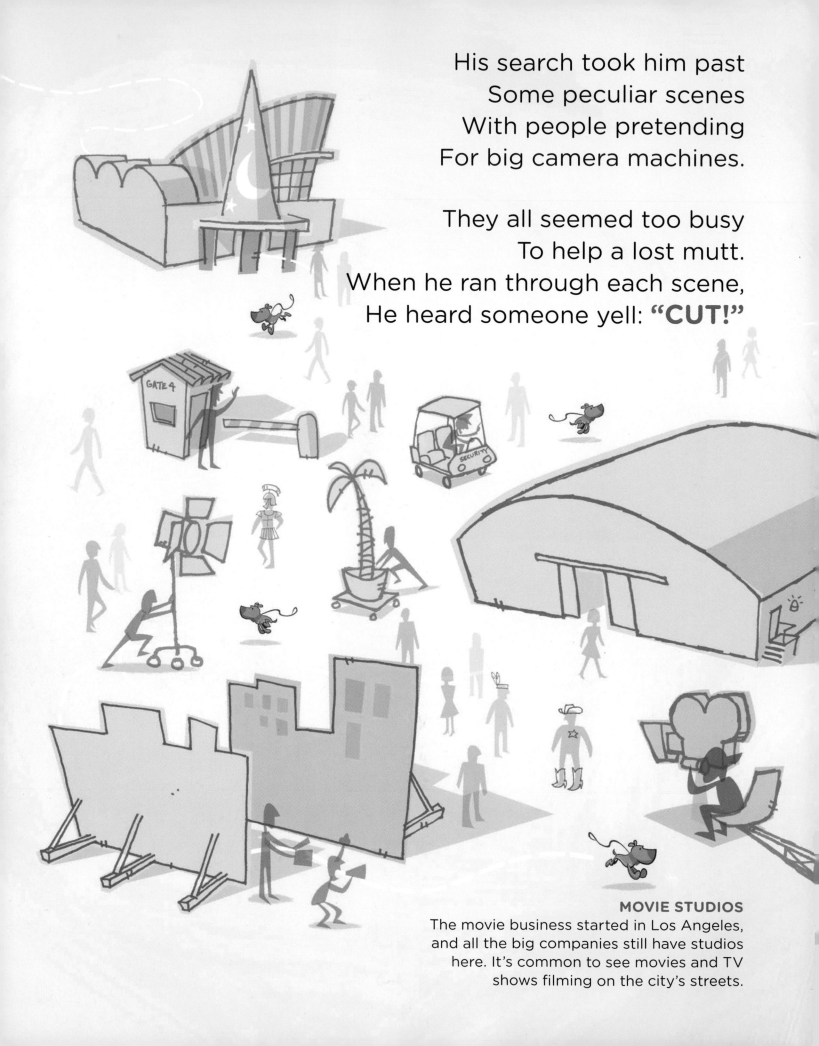

His search took him past
Some peculiar scenes
With people pretending
For big camera machines.

They all seemed too busy
To help a lost mutt.
When he ran through each scene,
He heard someone yell: **"CUT!"**

MOVIE STUDIOS
The movie business started in Los Angeles,
and all the big companies still have studios
here. It's common to see movies and TV
shows filming on the city's streets.

It seemed that everyone
Everywhere was out to get him.
Even a **fish with big jaws**—
But Larry didn't let him.

UNIVERSAL STUDIOS TOUR
The famous studio tour has been thrilling visitors
since 1964. Tourists ride a tram through floods,
earthquakes, and a real working movie studio.

Soon he found himself high up on a hill
Where a building stood set apart, quiet and still.

From the domed roof a **telescope** pointed up high.
This was clearly a place for those searching the sky.

MERCURY   VENUS   EARTH   MARS   JUPITER

GRIFFITH OBSERVATORY
Since opening in 1935, more people have looked through the observatory's telescope than any other telescope in the world.

SATURN

URANUS

NEPTUNE

One building he saw had
Tremendous appeal.
It was big and shiny,
Like **waves of steel.**

He heard beautiful music
Playing within,
But outside a strange dog
Looked back at him.

WALT DISNEY CONCERT HALL
This home to the L.A.
Philharmonic Orchestra was
designed by Frank Gehry and
is covered in stainless steel.

There were always more places
To search and explore.
From a **huge round building**
He heard a crowd roar.

He ran past the fans
All dressed in blue
Hoping that Pete might be
Cheering there, too.

DODGER STADIUM
Built in 1962, a few years after the Dodgers
moved from Brooklyn, New York, this
stadium has hosted eight World Series.

One of the busier streets he found
Had markets and history all around.

The people bustling here and there
Put a feel of **fiesta** in the air.

OLVERA STREET
This Mexican marketplace in the oldest part of downtown boasts 27 historic buildings.

A truck of treats made
Larry's eyes go wide.
With no sign of Pete,
He just hitched a ride.

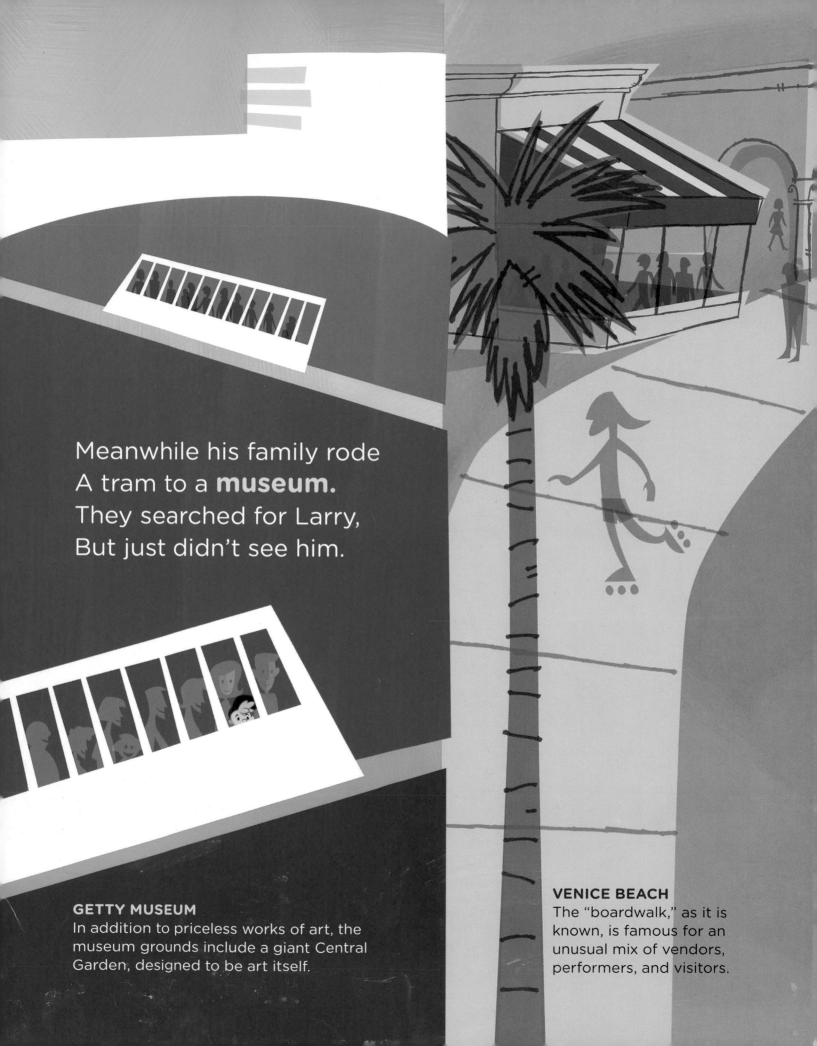

Meanwhile his family rode
A tram to a **museum.**
They searched for Larry,
But just didn't see him.

GETTY MUSEUM
In addition to priceless works of art, the museum grounds include a giant Central Garden, designed to be art itself.

VENICE BEACH
The "boardwalk," as it is known, is famous for an unusual mix of vendors, performers, and visitors.

On a beach Larry saw **muscle-guys** lifting weights
And some folks with tattoos and others on skates.

A guitar-playing guy gave Larry some food.
He was helpful, though he thought
Everyone's name was "dude."

He read the dog's collar and sent a quick text.
Somehow Larry knew a reunion was next.

A little ways up that very same beach
Was a **fun-filled pier**—he saw Pete within reach!

He ran up and jumped up and licked his pal's face.
Pete held tight onto his leash (just in case).

SANTA MONICA PIER
The pier, which opened in 1909, has a
full amusement park that includes the
landmark Ferris Wheel.

Pete shared with Larry the things he had seen,
And wondered out loud just where Larry had been.
Then they fell fast asleep as the car drove away.
It had been quite an **adventurous day.**

The
ADWAY
LYWOOD

EL CAPITAN

HOLLYWOOD

Hollywood

WAX MUSEUM

RANDY'S
DONUTS

Musso & Fra
Grill
Since 1919

Believe It or Not!
ODDITORIUM

BEVERLY
HILLS

OPEN